"Grandma, You Found Me!"

Deanna Nowadnick

Illustrations by Ben Young

Rhododendron Books • Monroe, Washington

"Grandma, You Found Me!"

Copyright © 2024 by Deanna Nowadnick

Printed and bound in the United States of America. All rights reserved. No part of this book may be reproduced or transmitted in any form or by any means, electronic or mechanical, including photocopying, recording, or by any information storage and retrieval system—except by a reviewer who may quote brief passages in a review to be printed in a magazine, newspaper, or on the internet without permission in writing from the publisher. For information, please contact Rhododendron Books, 703 Alden Avenue, Monroe, WA 98272.

Scripture quotation is from Contemporary English Version (CEV).
Copyright © 1995 by American Bible Society. It is shared with permission.

ISBN: 978-0-9835897-7-8

Library of Congress Control Number: 2024905995

Cover and Interior Art: Ben Young
Cover and Interior Design: Juanita Dix
Printed in the United State of America

To
Grandson Enzo

"Children are a blessing and a gift from the Lord."

–*Psalm 127:3 (CEV)*

Grandchildren too!

Love, Deanna

Grandma loved playdates with her grandson Henry.

Every week Grandma met Henry for afternoon fun.

She picked him up wherever he was.

Some weeks Henry was at preschool.

And Grandma picked him up for a walk to the park.

During summer months, Henry was at day camp.

One Wednesday Henry was playing tennis.

And Grandma picked him up for a picnic under the trees.

One week Henry was at soccer practice.

And Grandma picked him up after her last cheer for his last goal.

One afternoon Henry was at the swimming pool.
And when Henry saw Grandma, he shouted, "Grandma, you found me!"

Grandma smiled.
"Henry, I will always find you."

"I found you at school when you started kindergarten."

"I will find you at your soccer game this Saturday."

"We'll read your favorite book."

"I will find you at the airport when you travel."

"I will find you if you go to a new school in a new city in another state."

"Henry, I will even find you when you get bigger."

"We'll have our favorite snack in the sunshine."

"I will find you when you have your own house and your own family."

Heavenly Father,

Thank You for the gift of children. Grandchildren too!

May they always know they are loved, not just by grandparents, but by You.

In the name of Your dear Son Jesus, amen.

Other Books by Deanna Nowadnick

Fruit of My Spirit: Reframing Life in God's Grace

Signs in Life: Finding Direction in Our Travels with God

Bouquet of Wisdom: Reflections from the Garden

 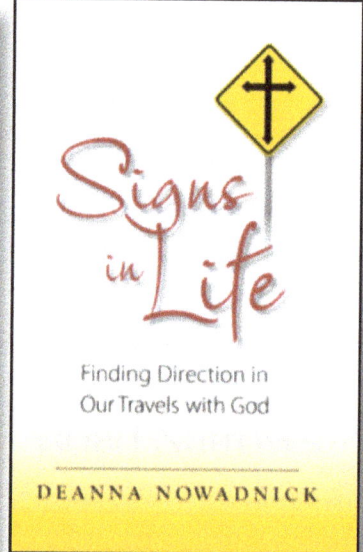 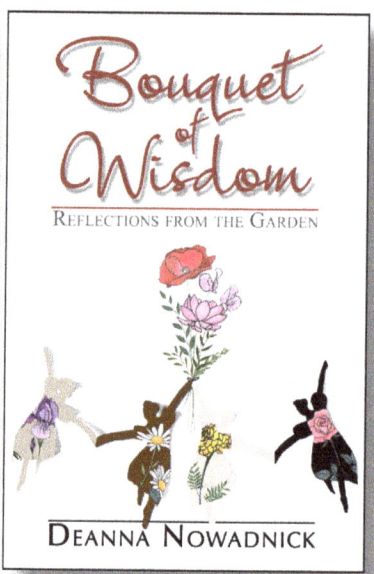

Printed in the USA
CPSIA information can be obtained
at www.ICGtesting.com
CBHW041230070424
6448CB00004B/10